FORBIDDEN TOWERS

Carol Gaskin

illustrations by T. Alexander Price

Library of Congress Cataloging-in-Publication Data

Gaskin, Carol.
  The forbidden towers.

  (The Forgotten forest)
  Summary: As Lifin, a young elf, the reader makes
decisions controlling his search through the five
Forbidden Towers for the herb that will cure his people
of the elven plague.
    1. Children's stories, American.   2. Plot-your-own
stories.   [1. Fantasy.   2. Plot-your-own stories]
I. Price, T. Alexander, ill.   II. Title.   III. Series:
Gaskin, Carol.   Forgotten forest.
PZ7.G213Fo   1985   [Fic]   84-16219
ISBN 0-8167-0324-8 (lib. bdg.)
ISBN 0-8167-7597-4 (pbk.)

This edition published in 2003.

Printed in Canada.

10 9 8 7 6 5 4 3 2 1

Welcome to the Forgotten Forest

In this adventure you are Lifin, a carefree young elf. Carefree, that is, until you must enter the Forbidden Towers.

As you read, you will be asked to make important decisions: Which of the five towers will you choose? Will you enter the Tower of Bones? Or the Tower of Hands? Will you speak to the sphinx in the Tower of Beasts? Or face the dangers in the Tower of Spiders?

There are many paths you can follow in the Forgotten Forest. You may end up as dinner in the Tower of Eaters—or you may save all of your people. The choice is yours.

When one adventure ends, you can always return to the beginning and follow a new path. Choose well, and the best of luck in your journey!

Wilderberries! At last! Clapping your hands in triumph, you leap high into the air and land lightly, right in the middle of the berry patch. You pop a fat, purple berry into your mouth and crush it with your tongue. It is perfect!

Won't the villagers be pleased, you think. You imagine them running to greet you. "Thank you, Lifin!" they cry. "The wilderberry quest is won!" "Hooray for young Lifin, finest of elves!"

You begin to pluck the ripe, juicy berries, tossing them one by one into the baskets you brought along— pausing frequently to reward your labors with a sweet, fruity mouthful.

Elves adore wilderberries, and the only patch near your village has been picked clean for months. Vowing to find a fresh supply, you set out to comb the forest. But even with your keen elven eyesight and acute sense of smell, it has taken many days of searching in the dense thickets beyond the forest paths before your patience was rewarded.

Sweeping your pale hair behind your pointed ears, you work cheerfully until your baskets are brimming. Then, memorizing your surroundings so you can find this patch again, you set off briskly through the forest, eager to present the village with your bountiful harvest.

When you emerge from the forest, you are pleased to see that you are not far from your village. The Forbidden Towers loom ahead.

"Spiders, Hands, Bones, Eaters, Beasts, *begone!*" you mutter as you approach the towers, drawing a five-pointed star in the air to enforce the simple charm you have recited all of your life.

Ancient and mysterious, the Forbidden Towers rise from the soft grass of the Great Meadow. Their cold, gray stone is an eerie contrast to the green field that flowers in an eternal elven spring.

The five towers have stood for as long as any elf can remember, and it has always been strictly forbidden to so much as touch one of the worm-eaten wooden doors.

A stone arch frames each of the five doors, and the keystone of each great arch bears a carved symbol. No one knows what the strange symbols really mean. But it is by these symbols that generations of young elves have known the towers: Spiders, Hands, Bones, Eaters, and Beasts.

You can remember joining hands with your play-
mates and circling the towers, passing each carving
and chanting its name. "Spiders, Hands, Bones,
Eaters, Beasts, *begone!*" you would sing, always
careful not to draw too close to the doors, for scary
stories were told at bedtime about foolish elves who
entered the towers, never to return.

You think of the games you have played in the
Great Meadow, and the lessons you have practiced
there. It was here you were taught to use a bow and
arrow, to make the elven spark, and to disappear.
You notice with surprise that no young elves are
playing in the meadow on such a fine day. Where is
everyone?

Sensing that something is wrong, you hurry past
the towers toward your village. Suddenly a voice calls
out to you.

"Lifin, stop! Come no closer! Do not enter the
village!"

It is Elvir, the Eldest of Elders. He stands at the
far edge of the Great Meadow, gesturing for you to
stay away. You freeze in mid-step. Elvir looks weak,
almost transparent. His long white hair flutters to his
waist, blending with the thin fabric of his tunic.
Both his voice and his image seem faded, drained of
strength.

"What is wrong, Master Elvir?" you call. Resisting an urge to run to his side, you keep your distance. Elvir, by virtue of his wisdom, has reached the rank of Elf of Greatest Substance, and you respectfully obey his wishes. "Why may I not enter my own village?" you ask. "I have brought wilderberries enough for all."

"Listen to me, Lifin, for I weaken quickly." Elvir's voice floats sadly across the meadow, a ghostly whisper.

"A plague has swept through our village, and all of elvenkind lie asleep, fading. Soon I shall sleep as well. I have waited for your return, for you are our only hope. Listen carefully:

"The tales of our ancestors tell of this plague. It visits elvenkind once every nine hundred years. It is said that there is an antidote—the only cure—a rare leafy plant. It is said that it grows only at the center of the Forbidden Towers." Elvir sighs.

"The towers must be filled with dangerous enchantments, Lifin. According to our legends, known only to the Elders, the Forbidden Towers were created by one of our own, an elven magician named Zandea.

"During the last time of plague, Zandea built the Towers to protect the plant from our enemies. But in his zeal to protect the cure for our slumbering people, and in his haste to build the towers, he grew weak. Zandea neglected to take the antidote himself. He was lost to the plague, and the secret route to the center of the towers was lost with him. You will have to find it on your own."

Elvir pauses for breath. "Little about the Towers is known, but I can tell you this," he continues. "Take no weapons inside, Lifin, for they will only hinder you. You must rely on your special *elven* qualities to help you in your quest. You have studied hard, and you have learned your lessons well. You can leap high into the air. If you click your fingers you can make the elven spark. And you are able to disappear."

Elvir's voice begins to waver as he labors to speak.

"But be forewarned, Lifin. If you choose to disappear while you are within the Forbidden Towers, the act will drain your energy, leaving you momentarily weak. And you will reappear in one of the four other towers. But which one, and where, will be beyond your control."

Elvir shimmers and begins to fade.

"I must rest. Good luck, Lifin," he says. "Search for the center, and find the healing herb." Then he is gone.

Slowly you lower your baskets of wilderberries to the ground. Unfastening your cherished bow and quiverful of arrows, you place them beside the baskets. Then you face the Forbidden Towers.

You decide to walk around the gloomy towers and study the doors, as you have done so often on more carefree days.

"Spiders, Hands, Bones, Eaters, Beasts, *begone!*" you say out of habit as you regard each tower, feeling slightly foolish, for you know that the weak charm spoken by superstitious elf children will offer you little protection against what may lie within.

You can still make out the carved spider on the first weathered keystone. One of its delicate forelegs is raised as though it is about to spring from its web.

The Tower of Hands bears an open palm on its keystone. The Tower of Bones has a skull and crossbones. A crossed knife and fork mark the Tower of Eaters. And a monstrous face decorates the Tower of Beasts.

Gathering your courage for the perilous adventure before you, you circle the Forbidden Towers once more. This time you choose a door and enter.

If you enter the Tower of Spiders, turn to page 24.

If you enter the Tower of Hands, turn to page 40.

If you enter the Tower of Bones, turn to page 60.

If you enter the Tower of Eaters, turn to page 48.

If you enter the Tower of Beasts, turn to page 32.

10

You wander into a small forest. Ahead of you is a small cottage. It looks so familiar, so much like home, that you enter without a thought.

Indoors, a wooden table is set with four places, and three steaming bowls of porridge. A young girl with long blonde ringlets carries a fourth steaming bowl to the table.

"There you are, you naughty bear!" she says, wagging a finger at you. A glance into a nearby mirror confirms your fear—you now have the head and paws of a bear. The girl continues her scolding.

"I can see that you've been over the river and through the wood. You're covered with mud. You probably got all the way to Grandmother's house before you realized you'd forgotten the basket of goodies, right? Well, here it is. That poor old soul is probably half starved by now. And you must be, too. Now sit down and eat your porridge."

You seem to have stumbled into the story of "The Three Bears." But Goldilocks certainly isn't as sweet as you thought she would be. And this story is all twisted and confused!

If you sit down and eat your porridge, turn to page 110.

If you'd rather deliver the basket to Grandmother's house, turn to page 19.

You land, slightly stunned, in a walled courtyard filled with palm trees.

Ahead of you is a heavy door. Behind you, leading away from the courtyard, are five narrow alleys.

You explore each fingerlike alley in turn, but all are dead ends. Finally you understand. You have landed in a *palm* court, shaped like an outstretched hand. You are in the Tower of Hands!

You try the door.

Turn to page 40.

12

The chugging noise slows, then stops, as you turn the fist-shaped doorknob of the first room. The knob feels warm, like a living hand, and it pulls from your grip as the door opens.

You step into a private railroad car! Empty rows of wooden seats, carved like cupped hands, line a central aisle. The walls are paneled, and hung with velvet draperies. There are potted palms flanking the doorway. And the aisle is lit by globes of white light, hung from the walls and ceiling by hand-shaped mounts.

You can still hear the dull pounding sound you noticed outside. It grows louder as you walk the length of the car, toward a door at the opposite end.

Pausing at a pair of seats to peer behind the heavy drapes, you are surprised to see your reflection gazing back at you. Windows! Pressing your face to the glass, you try to block out the inside light with your hands. You can see nothing but darkness beyond.

Suddenly, with a loud screech, the car lurches forward and throws you into one of the seats. The chugging noise begins again, building slowly—and the car feels as if it's moving!

If you stay in your seat to see what happens, turn to page 22.

If you run for the door at the end of the car, turn to page 86.

You begin to climb across the boulders. It is a long way to the earth mound, but the climb is easier than you thought it would be. The closer to the mound you get, the smoother and flatter the rocks become, until they are almost perfectly oval.

You pause atop a rounded boulder to survey your progress. Suddenly the rock jolts beneath your feet, throwing you off balance. Tumbling onto your back, you stare as the huge boulder splits and opens. Inside it is a pale and delicate pink, and at its center rests a perfect pearl, as large as your head!

Another boulder creaks and opens, and yet another. Each holds a pearl, lustrous and moonlike. These smooth rocks are giant oysters!

The earth mound looms before you, a stronghold of the unknown. Who knows whom you might meet? Perhaps you should bring a pearl to use as a bribe— or as a weapon.

If you decide to stop and take a pearl, turn to page 43.

If you go directly to the earth mound, turn to page 26.

14

You decide to try the iron door. Such a strong door must be shielding something important, you think. Perhaps you will find a passageway to the center of the towers.

The heavy door swings open easily. Inside it is dark. Removing a burning torch from a wall bracket, you enter cautiously. The iron door slams shut behind you.

You hear a strange purring noise. Your torchlight picks out, in a corner of the room, four pairs of glowing eyes. And they all belong to a gigantic, hairy tarantula!

You take a step backward as the huge spider rears up on his hind legs. Each of his legs ends in a vicious claw.

You wave the flaming torch back and forth. The tarantula opens his powerful jaws, revealing a fearsome set of fangs. As he shifts to one side, perhaps to attack, you can see that he guards some sort of tunnel.

Do tarantulas eat elves? you wonder. You have heard that tarantulas are poisonous. But you have also heard that they make fine pets.

If you want to try to tame the tarantula, turn to page 56.

If you want to make a run for the tunnel, turn to page 36.

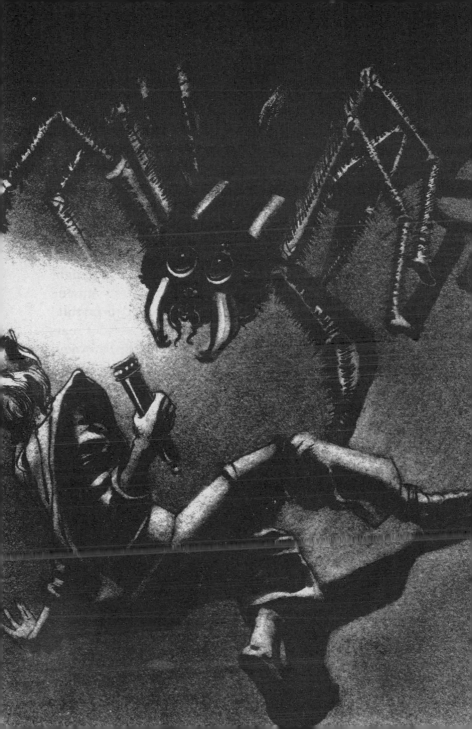

16

You decide to use the power in your own hands to fight off these devilish gloves.

Whoosh! One flies past your face and tickles your nose. *Crash!* Another drops a glass bottle that breaks at your feet.

Gathering together the fingertips on your left hand, you brush them lightly with your thumb. *Zzzzzt!* An elven spark leaps from your fingers. The spark stuns a glove, and it falls to the floor. *Zzzzzt!* Two more—and the white gloves flurry like confused moths. They group on the ceiling around a crystal chandelier.

You retreat to the door and escape to the hallway. Slamming the door behind you, you hear the noise of breaking glass as the huge chandelier shatters on the floor.

You had better continue your quest in a different room.

If you choose the first door, turn to page 12.

If you choose the second door, turn to page 34.

from page 108

You focus all of your energies on the image of a spiral seashell. Closing your eyes, you picture yourself spiraling away.

You emerge from your sleeplike state feeling weak. You are in a barren chamber, empty except for two wall-mirrors, one on each side of the room.

Seeing your reflection, you jump! Then you struggle to your feet, looking from one mirror to the other and back again. In the first mirror, you have the head and paws of a bear. In the second mirror you wear a fox's head. You must be in the Tower of Beasts!

Approaching a mirror, you timidly press a toe against the silvered surface. Your toe seems to melt right through the mirror.

Yanking your toe back into the chamber, you rest until your elven energy is restored. Then you resume your quest.

If you pass through the mirror that reflects you with a bear's head, turn to page 10.

If you pass through the "fox" mirror, turn to page 45.

18

You are in a weaver's shop. The room is clean, with shiny wooden floors and a high beamed ceiling. Skeins of wool, dyed many colors, overflow from baskets in the center of the room. Lengths of cloth are draped on wooden racks along one wall. Along another are vats of dye, tufts of unspun wool, and spinning wheels.

You realize that someone is working on the huge loom that takes up most of the far corner of the room, for you can hear the rhythmic clacking of the shuttle and treadles.

Crossing to the loom, you see that the weaver is a thin old woman dressed in a gown of gossamer gray. She greets you with a smile.

"Here for a fitting, young elf? I am famous for my elven cloaks. Come, I have one just your size." She hops nimbly from her bench and you follow her to the racks of fabric.

"Try this one," she says, offering you a silver-green cloak.

It is the most beautiful garment you have ever seen, silky and lustrous, with an intricate pattern of grasses and dewdrops, insects and wildflowers.

If you accept the cloak, turn to page 28.

If you refuse the old woman's handiwork, turn to page 41.

You decide you'd better get out of here before Mama Bear and Papa Bear come home.

"I'll deliver the basket right now," you tell Goldilocks, "while my porridge cools."

"Very well," answers the crabby girl. "Only don't look inside, or you'll spoil your dinner."

Taking the basket with its cheerful covering of blue-and-white-checked cloth, you set off through the forest. You are well on your way to Grandmother's house when you come face to face with a horrible laughing beast.

A manticore! It has the face of a man, the body of a lion, and a scorpion's tail. The manticore sings in a voice as grating as a rooster's first cry:

> *"A tisket, a tasket*
> *A bear bearing a basket!*
> *You're curious to look inside,*
> *No matter how you mask it!"*

Then he shrieks with ear-splitting glee. "Let's see what's in the basket! Go ahead, open it up, you cowardly bear!"

If you oblige the manticore and open the basket, turn to page 116.

If you obey Goldilocks, and don't look inside, turn to page 113.

from page 60/from page 76

You decide to try the staircase blocked by the pile of fish bones.

The delicate ribs look as sharp as porcupine quills, so you pick your way gingerly into the heap.

Suddenly you hear a throaty growl, like that of an angry cat.

Yiiahhmeeow! With a shrill howl, the skeleton of a snarling wildcat bounds down the staircase and springs at you!

If you leap out of the way, turn to page 33.

If you throw an armload of fish bones at the attacking skeleton, turn to page 49.

from page 119

You are too weak to disappear, so you decide to stall for time by entertaining the laughing ogres.

You struggle to your feet and juggle some potatoes. The ogres stare in amazement, then begin to clap and guffaw.

As your energy returns, you start to sing and dance on the table, hopping nimbly among the goblets and silverware. The ogres stomp their feet and pound their fists in time to your rollicking tune.

Next you tell the story of the bearded dragon and his fire-breathing wife. The ogres slap their knees, and tears of mirth spill from their eyes. Even the servants clearing the banquet table laugh until they cry.

You tell story after story, each topping the last. Finally you tell your funniest tale, the story of the mammoth who trumpeted lions from his trunk. The lions roared men, who in turn spoke frogs, who croaked locusts. Before you have finished, the ogres are rolling on the floor, clutching their bellies and whooping with delight.

In the confusion, you hop into an urn that a servant is clearing away. And, still laughing, the servant pours you down a chute.

Turn to page 122.

22

Judging by the chugging sounds, you are on a moving train! You decide to see where it will take you.

You are sitting in the cupped palm of a huge wooden hand, your back against four well-padded fingers, and your arm resting on a curled thumb.

Your window looks out into pitch darkness and reflects your face in the yellow light thrown by two globes, each perched on the palm of a bronze hand.

In a pocket on the back of the seat in front of you, you find a thick book, *HANDbook for Travelers*. Thumbing through its many pages, you see that it lists one thousand possible routes through the Forbidden Towers. Searching for some mention of a magical herb, you pause at the word "jungle."

All at once the thumb armrest uncurls and springs across your lap, clamping you into your seat. You are trapped!

The view from your window changes. You pass through a desert littered with white bones, and a jungle overgrown with devouring plants, into the mouth of a silver-tusked boar, out through a spider-filled cavern, and back to the darkness of the Tower of Hands. There is no sign of the herb you are looking for.

You struggle in your seat, but to no avail. You consult the *HANDbook* again. You have another nine hundred ninety-nine trips to choose from. You hope you can find the magic plant in time.

THE END

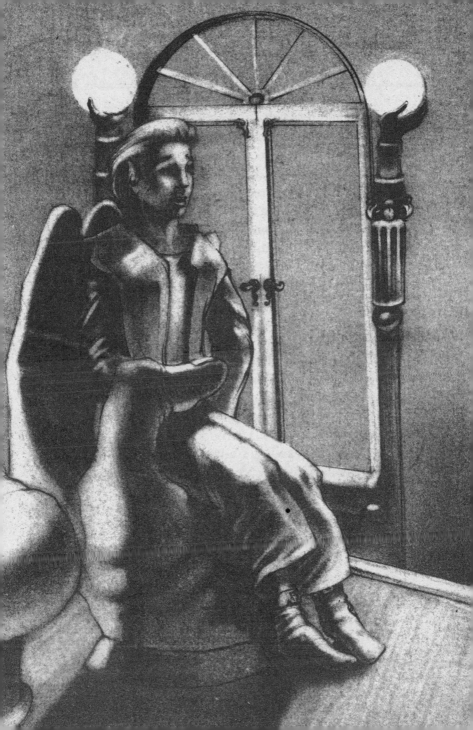

24

from page 9

You choose the dust-heavy door to the Tower of Spiders. The door creaks on its hinges, disturbing a cat's cradle of cobwebs.

You step into a dim, stuffy room, thick with centuries of webbing and dust, like layers of tattered cheesecloth. You sneeze from the dust, and try to brush the sticky cobwebs from your nose and eyelashes and hair. Something is tickling the back of your neck, and you slap at it with a shiver.

Suddenly the tangle of cobwebs begins to twitch and pull, and you notice movement everywhere you look. In every web, on walls and floor, the room is filled with little spiders!

The spiders look harmless enough, you think. But you would like to get out of this suffocating room. To your left, a stone staircase leads up into the tower. Ahead of you is a passageway, with a door dimly visible at the end.

A spider is crawling on your arm! Knocking it to the floor, you blink—twice. Is it your imagination, or are the tiny spiders creeping ever closer?

With your hands shielding your face, you run ahead through the webs.

If you head up the staircase, turn to page 106.

If you run through the door at the end of the passageway, turn to page 18.

You make a running leap to the rooftop of the Tower of Eaters, narrowly missing one of the jagged teeth around its edge.

The yeti roars after you, waving his arms from the Tower of Beasts.

It is too late to heed his warning. The roof you have just landed on is wet and soft, like a giant tongue. Before you can spring away, the teeth close around you, and you are swallowed by the rooftop mouth.

Turn to page 119.

from page 13

Reminding yourself that you are in the Tower of Eaters, you decide to leave the pearls behind. You don't want to be digested by a giant oyster! Certain that your quest lies within the earth mound, you pass through a final stand of trees.

Next to the massive mound you suddenly feel very small. The door alone is taller than the trees, and the mound itself rises far up the tower walls.

The great door splits and opens. This time you are reminded even more of a huge mouth, for a bright red carpet rolls out of the jawlike gates, unfurling at your feet like a giant tongue.

Accepting the invitation, and summoning all your courage, you follow the carpet through the gates of the earth mound and into a dank hallway.

The doors thunder closed and a rumbling echo fills the hall. Your eyes soon adjust to the darkness, but the echo does not die out. The rumble is growing louder. You look behind you. The carpet!

The heavy carpet is rolling toward you, growing larger with every turn, like a scarlet snowball. You must run or you'll be crushed.

Down the endless hallway you run, chased by the relentless rolling tongue. Soon the hallway ends. You see two large holes in the floor ahead. The first hole is lined with metal. Beads of moisture cling to its edge, and it looks slippery. The second hole is dry, and seems to be padded with colorful quilts. The carpet is upon you. You must jump!

If you jump into the first hole, turn to page 119.

If you choose the second hole, turn to page 108.

from page 18

Taking the shimmering cloak from the old woman, you drape it about your shoulders. It is a perfect fit and feels cozier the longer you wear it.

You admire your reflection in a tall oval mirror nearby. Behind you, the old woman is smiling her approval. You are as snug as a bug in a—*web!* The cloak is becoming a strong silken spider's web. As you struggle to free yourself, it binds you tighter.

"A *perfect* fit," gloats the old woman. Her spindly arms and bony legs grow longer and thinner, and four more legs unfold from her gray gown. As she changes into a leering gray spider, she hums a happy tune. You recognize the tune as "The Widow's Waltz," from the human operetta, *The Merry Widow*.

A widow! One of the most poisonous of all spiders!

You think you can burn through the silken threads of the web with the elven spark. But you would still be alone with the widow. Or you can disappear— and wind up who knows where?

If you try to use the elven spark to break out of the widow's web, turn to page 77.

If you choose to disappear, turn to page 44.

from page 98

You see yet another hand reaching for you through the sassafras leaves. Gathering your fingertips together to make a single surface, you brush them with your thumb. *Zzzzzt!* A sizzling spark flies from your fingers, striking the open palm of the sassafras hand.

The elven spark seems to sting the grabber, for it curls in on itself, scratching at its palm with its pearly fingernails.

Zzzzzt! Zzzzzt! Quickly you send two more sparks. The hand gripping your ankle opens wide as it is stung. You send still more sparks at the stunned grabber on your shoulder. It, too, releases you and you drop to the ground.

Leaping to the garden door, you escape to the hallway, a wild army of ivy fingers pinching at your feet. You decide to continue your quest in a different room.

Moving down the hallway, you come to the first door in the Tower of Hands.

Turn to page 12.

30

Choosing the second staircase, you make your way to the mound of bones that blocks your path. With a graceful elven leap, you spring easily to the top of the pile, but you find yourself caught, ankle-deep in the jumble of rugged bones.

You are patiently digging yourself out of the pile, moving the hefty bones aside one at a time, when the great heap begins to rattle and shake. Some of the bones fly into the air, clattering and connecting like the pieces of some mad machine. They are reassembling!

Before you can decide what to do next, the skeleton of a lame jackal is bounding at you, his fangs bared!

Lame? You realize that you are holding a canine leg bone—one of the jackal's. Can you defend yourself with it?

If you conk the jackal on the head, turn to page 76.

If you try to lodge the bone upright between the jackal's gaping jaws, turn to page 121.

from page 9

You decide to begin your quest in the Tower of Beasts.

The walls of this tower have always impressed you. But today is the first time you've studied them carefully. As you gaze up to the tower's snow-white peak, a gust of wind disturbs its outline against the sky. You can see that the snowy covering is actually a thick coat of white fur.

The door to the tower shimmers and turns silver as you approach. You are greeted by your own reflection, thin and pale, with hair as silver as the tower door.

There is no doorknob. But as you press against the silvered door, your limbs slip silently through its surface, fingers through reflected fingers, nose through mirrored nose. You are inside.

Within the Tower of Beasts is a single chamber, containing two panels. Before you stand two bestial warriors, one with the head of a bear, the other with the head of a fox. You jump into an elven posture of self-defense. The warriors do likewise.

With a nervous laugh, you realize your mistake: You are facing two mirrored panels. But in one mirror you have the head and paws of a bear. And in the other, you see Lifin the fox-headed. The rest of you is still elven.

If you pass through the mirror in which you wear a bear's head, turn to page 10.

If you pass through the mirror in which you wear a fox's head, turn to page 45.

from page 20

Leaping to your left, you land on the staircase just as the hollow-eyed wildcat pounces onto the pile of fish bones. You watch, frozen, as the bones snap and crackle, then disintegrate to a heap of sparkling dust.

Hissing angrily, the skeleton cat slinks toward you, sniffing at your feet. You back slowly up the staircase, wondering what to do next.

Ready to strike, stretched almost full-length on its bony belly, the skeleton cat sniffs at you again.

It relaxes! Apparently satisfied that you are not a tasty fish, it trots back to its pile of fish dust!

Breathing a sigh of relief, you pass safely up the staircase as the skeleton cat circles three times, then settles into its dusty bed for a nap.

Turn to page 95.

34

You do not know what "Grabbers" are, but perhaps they will lead you to the healing herb. You choose the second door.

Taking the hand that serves as a doorknob, you spell "Open, please," in the sign language of the Earless, peaceful neighbors of your elven village. The doorknob grips your hand in a firm handshake, then twists to open the door.

You step into a walled garden in what must be the center of the Tower of Hands. Fruit-bearing trees and hedges groomed in animal shapes line white-pebbled paths. Flowers are everywhere.

The garden walls rise many stories above you, to the top of the tower. On the far wall, a trellis of roses climbs to a great clock face. And there seems to be an oval window beneath the numeral twelve.

You wander among the flower beds, studying the clock and searching for an unfamiliar herb. Finally you reach the center of the garden. Perhaps the magical plant is concealed among more common plants, you think. Kneeling by the edge of the path, you part a group of leafy snapdragon stalks to look for hidden herbs.

Something nips at your shoulders! At your ears!

Jumping back in surprise, you see that the snap-dragon blossoms have all turned to tiny hands—and they are growing larger, and snapping at you. Grabbers!

Throughout the garden, fruits and flowers are turning into hands. The pears, the peonies, and the roses on the trellis are all straining on their stems or vines, reaching for you.

Soon you will have trouble getting through this garden of grabbers. You see only two ways to escape.

If you try to scale the wall to the clock, turn to page 80.

If you try to leap your way back to the door, turn to page 98.

from page 14

The rearing tarantula doesn't look friendly. You decide to try to hold him off with your torch until you can make a run for the tunnel.

Slowly, you begin to circle the eight-legged beast, hoping to get closer to the tunnel entrance. The tarantula drops back down onto his front legs. Suddenly a hairy leg swipes at your torch! But your elven agility is a match for the giant spider's, and you nimbly toss the blazing torch from your right hand to your left, and back again.

The tarantula's eight eyes move back and forth, following the torchlight as you switch hands. Perhaps I can hypnotize this spider, you think, gradually slowing your rhythm. The tarantula falls completely still, moving only his eyes. He seems to be getting sleepy.

You shift your gaze sideways, trying to gauge your distance from the tunnel. But in the split second your eyes look away, the spider attacks! Before you know what is happening, the tarantula catches your torch in one crablike claw, and lifts you in another!

As he draws you toward his glistening fangs, you struggle to escape. It is no use. He bites your arm, and drops you to the floor. Then he casually moves away to anchor the torch in a wall bracket.

Now I'll be paralyzed, you think desperately, and the spider will eat me. Waiting to feel the effects of the poison, you remember hearing tales of a frantic dance, the tarantella, that some people believe wears off the effects of a tarantula's bite.

Dancing may be worth a try—but should you dance here, or first risk using your strength in order to disappear?

If you dance the tarantella right where you are, turn to page 82.

If you choose to disappear, turn to page 99.

from page 97

You decide to put on the suit of armor before you enter the next room. You can always remove it later if you have to.

Carefully placing your pearl on the floor of the storeroom, you dismantle the armor and begin to climb into it piece by piece.

It is no easy task, for you feel clumsier with each part you strap on. The breastplate is heavy, the greaves are cumbersome, the gauntlets are awkward. Finally, as you lower the helmet onto your head, the visor snaps closed!

Finding it stuffy and hard to see, you try to open the steel-plated face guard, but your fingers just won't bend in the inflexible gauntlets.

Trying to pull one gauntlet off with the other, you find they are both stuck.

You pull at each bulky piece, but the suit of armor is sealed tightly at every joint. You are trapped in elf-eating armor!

Then you feel the tiny teeth that spring from the inside of your armored suit. Your quest ends in the Tower of Eaters.

THE END

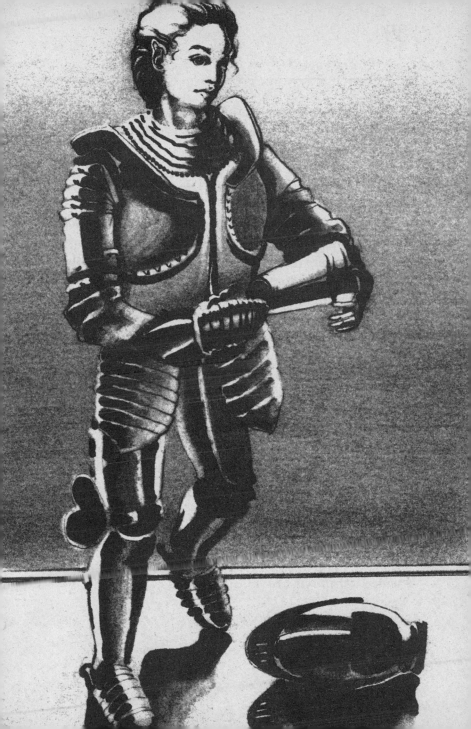

40

The door swings open of its own accord, and you enter the Tower of Hands. As though pushed by unseen hands, the door slams shut behind you.

A narrow hallway leads straight ahead. Torches held by lifelike hands extend from one wall, lighting three doorways.

You press your ear to the first door. You hear a thick chugging noise, like that of a great machine inside and a hollow pounding in the background. One of the hands suddenly dips its torch to point invitingly at the fist-shaped doorknob.

Moving to the second door, you pause to watch a silent message spelled in rapid symbols by a slender hand. In its gestures, you recognize the language of the Earless, peaceful creatures who make their homes in the Forgotten Forest. "Beware—Grabbers," spells the hand. The room beyond is silent.

At the third door, a crooked finger extends through a keyhole and beckons you to enter. You can hear soft whistling sounds behind the door, like distant fireworks.

If you enter the first room, turn to page 12.

If you enter the second room, turn to page 34.

If you enter the third room, turn to page 92.

Although it is tempting, you refuse the beautiful cloak. After all, you are in the Tower of Spiders, and it pays to be careful.

"It is magnificent, but no thank you," you tell the woman in gray.

"Well, well, a *careful* little elf, aren't you?" says the old woman. "But perhaps I can change your mind."

As she stretches her arms toward you, you see that tiny claws have replaced her hands. In one claw she holds the glimmering cloak, and in the other a long, shiny sewing needle. Her arms grow spindly and sprout bristly hairs. And six long legs have sprung where once were only two! Her hairpins turn to eight dark eyes, and she speaks through glistening fangs.

"Won't you stay and keep a poor old widow company?" she croons in a silky voice.

A widow! The old woman has transformed into one of the most poisonous of all spiders!

You must defend yourself at once.

If you grab the sewing needle, turn to page 84.

If you grab the cloak, turn to page 114.

42

You set off for Grandmother's house, and wander into a small forest. Ahead of you is a small cottage. It looks *very* familiar.

"There you are, you naughty bear!" says a nagging voice.

Oh, no, you think. Goldilocks again. She appears, scowling, in the doorway.

"Come and eat your porridge this instant," she orders. "I want you tucked into bed before Mama Bear and Papa Bear get home."

You walk dutifully past Goldilocks and enter the cottage once again.

"And where is my good basket?" she is saying. "Have you lost another one of my best picnic baskets?"

You decide to shut your ears as best you can and eat while you have the chance. The porridge smells delicious.

Turn to page 110.

You are fascinated by the giant oysters. The beautiful pearls appeal to your elven eyes, and they may be useful as well.

But you know a trap when you see one. This *is* the Tower of Eaters after all, and you don't intend to become dinner for an oyster. You decide you had better prop open an oyster shell before taking a pearl.

Searching the ground beneath the stand of trees, you soon find a hefty branch to use as a wedge. You jam the upright branch into an oyster so that it can't close.

When you are satisfied that the branch will hold, you step into the oyster shell. It is slippery! You slide along its slick surface, gaining speed until you collide with the large pearl at its center. Carefully, you pick it up.

Slipping and sliding, you make your way out of the shell with the pearl tucked under your arm. It is as heavy as a ripe melon, and as white as Elvir's beard.

Should you collect another pearl before venturing into the earth mound?

If you decide to take a second pearl, turn to page 68.

If you enter the earth mound with your single pearl, turn to page 97.

44

You close your eyes and imagine the inside of a spiral seashell. Gathering all of your energy, you soon feel yourself spiraling away.

When your eyelids flutter open again, your head is still spinning and you are too weak to move.

Gradually, you lift your head, for you realize that you are not alone. You have landed in a cage with massive iron bars. You must be in the Tower of Beasts!

Your companion is a beast unknown to you. He paces the cage, walking upright, but sometimes dropping onto all fours. He never needs to turn around, for he has two heads, one at each end of his body. He is feathered from head to hoof—for hooves he has—and he slowly changes color, from blue to bright orange.

"What *are* you?" you ask in amazement.

"A cambochrome," says the beast. "My feathers change color depending on my mood. For example, when I'm bored, my feathers turn blue."

"But how do you feel when they turn orange?" you ask.

"Hungry!"

THE END

A fox's head appeals to your elven nature more than a bear's. Passing through the "fox" panel, you arrive in a barren desert.

You felt no pain at all, but your hands are now a fox's paws, and your nose a furred snout.

Oh well, you think, being half fox is not so bad. Making the best of the situation, you set out to explore your surroundings.

You search the ground so carefully for signs of the magic herb that at first you don't notice the strange mound of sand just ahead of you. The mound shimmers in the desert heat.

You draw closer. It is a sphinx! Half woman, half lion, the ancient beast waits patiently for your approach, her wings folded neatly across her chest.

"Greetings, great Sphinx," you say.

"Greetings, Fox-head," she replies. "You have entered the Sands of the Sphinx, the Realm of the Riddle. It is my right to pose you one riddle. If you answer correctly, I will restore to you your true form. If you are incorrect, well, we shall see. If you refuse to answer, I shall devour you at once." You decide to answer as best you can.

"Here is my riddle," continues the sphinx. "What has two eyes, pointed ears, a long tail, and is the cleverest of beasts in the Tower?"

If you guess a fox, turn to page 51.

If you guess something else, turn to page 104.

48

from page 9

You approach the imposing door to the Tower of Eaters. Silently, the door splits in two and opens, the lower half sinking and the upper half rising like a gaping mouth. As you hop through the opening, the door crunches shut behind you.

To your surprise, you find yourself in a charming garden, full of trees, encircled by the walls of the tower and open to the sky.

At the back of the garden rises a moss-covered mound of earth. A door seems to be built into the side of the mound.

To your left, a path leads under an arbor of colorful flowers and winds away. Another path, to your right, leads to a quiet lake that reflects the mysterious mound.

You decide that the earth mound is as good a place as any to search for the plant that will heal your people. But a direct route to the mound is blocked by a thick patch of hawthorns and briars.

If you set off through the arbor, turn to page 72.

If you choose the path to the lake, turn to page 90.

from page 20

Grabbing a handful of fish bones, you hurl them at the wildcat's screaming skull.

To your horror, the fish bones crumble into dust. But the dust flies at the cat's skull. The skeleton cat lands at your feet and begins to cough and hiss. You leap up the staircase, leaving the guardian skeleton behind.

Turn to page 95.

50

It seems as though the raft has been waiting here just for you. Pleased with your luck, you push the raft afloat and hop aboard. Then, feeling for the bottom of the lake with your sapling pole, you push off. The lake is not deep and the raft moves steadily. You are on your way!

Finding you can control your small craft well enough to keep it off the rocks, you decide to be a cautious boatman and stay close to the shore.

You are bothered by a faint hissing noise that seems to rise from the water. You search the lake for snakes, but see nothing. Then you notice that the lake is gradually getting deeper—or your pole is getting shorter. It feels lighter in your grip.

Yanking the pole out of the lake, you are startled to see that it has partly fizzled away. And the hissing noise is coming from the underside of your raft.

Quickly tearing a piece of cloth from your shirt you drop it into the lake. *Pffizzzz.* You are afloat on a pool of acid!

The thongs binding your raft together fray and snap. The logs are coming apart!

Balancing on two disintegrating logs, you leap to the lakeside boulders, grateful that your reluctance to swim has kept you close to the shore.

Turn to page 13.

from page 47

The sphinx waits serenely as you ponder her riddle.

Two eyes, pointy ears, clever, long tail—what else could it be?

"A fox," you answer.

"Not so, Fox-head!" says the sphinx, smiling triumphantly. "You are the only fox in the Tower of Beasts, and you have not been clever enough to guess my riddle.

"We shall meet again in one year's time. Perhaps by then you will be able to answer me correctly."

The sphinx vanishes into the desert air and you, with the head of a fox, are left to wander for a year in the Tower of Beasts. But then it will be too late to save your village.

THE END

52

You are in a dim hallway, lit by candelabra that hang from the ceiling like upside-down spiders. You come to a curtain at the end of the hall. Beyond it, a chorus hums an eerie and monotonous song. Yet the music is strangely beautiful. You wonder what awaits you now in this part of the Tower of Spiders.

Drawing the curtain aside, you find yourself in a huge ballroom. The room is filled with a thousand spiders, dressed in white turbans and gowns, slowly moving in circles as they chant. You wander among them, but they do not seem to notice you.

The music builds and a few of the spiders begin to jump up and down. Like a roomful of popping corn, more and more spiders burst into jumping as the music heats up.

"We are the Jumping Dervishes," says a voice near your ear. "Please join our ceremony if you wish."

The music is growing faster and more intense, the circling dervishes are making you dizzy, and with your elven love of leaping, you long to join the dance. You search the ballroom for an exit, but you are completely surrounded by a maze of jumping spiders.

If you join the dervish dance, turn to page 71.

If you disappear, turn to page 22.

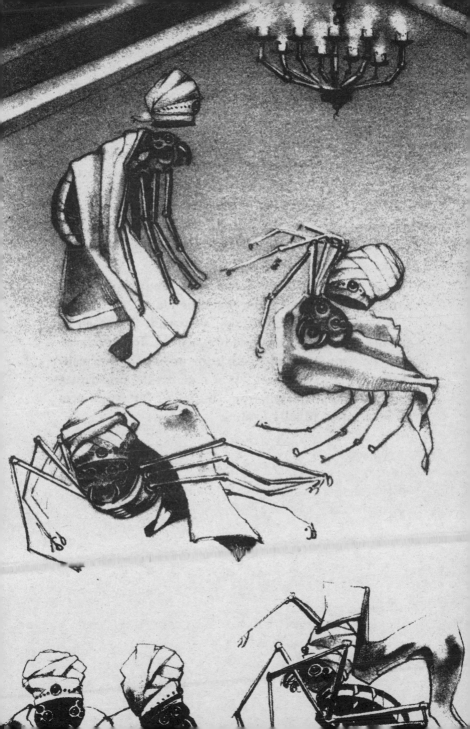

54

from page 72

You decide to use the elven spark against the hungry flowers. Pinching your nose tightly closed with one hand, you gather the fingertips of your other hand together to make a single smooth surface, then brush them with your thumb.

Zzzzt! A sizzling spark zings from your fingertips and strikes a purple and yellow elftrap as it nibbles on your sleeve. The heavy bloom stops chewing and flops over, stunned. The spark works!

Zzzzt! Zzzzt! In short order you break through the arbor, out of reach of the ravenous plants.

Seeing no more elftraps, you walk to the earth mound. But it is surrounded by a thick stone wall.

Wasting no time, you begin to climb the wall. Near the top, you throw an arm across the uppermost block to pull yourself over the edge. But your arm seems to stick in jelly.

Pulling yourself up onto the top of the wall, you see that a substance like raspberry jam has been spread on each block. It burbles and oozes. Your arm is now stuck and so is the rest of you.

You remain calm until you notice that the jelly has dissolved a hole in your boot. Your toes are beginning to tingle. Your only choice is to disappear *immediately*.

You concentrate on the image of a spiral seashell, and feel yourself spiraling away.

Turn to page 52.

You decide to see if the tarantula is tame. Perhaps he is frightened by the flame.

You stop waving your torch. After a moment, the tarantula closes his jaws and drops back to the floor. Standing quite still, he watches you with all eight of his eyes.

You hold the torch well away from the hairy spider, and take a few slow steps in his direction. He makes no move to attack you, so you draw closer. Then, reaching up, you gently pet his furry back.

"Nice tarantula," you say soothingly. "Don't eat me, please."

"Don't be silly," replies the spider. "Tarantulas don't eat elves. You just surprised me with that torch of yours."

"I'm sorry if I startled you," you say, quite startled yourself at meeting a talking tarantula. "I am searching for the center of the Forbidden Towers. Do you know where the tunnel behind you goes?"

"No, I'm just a guard, not an explorer," says the tarantula. "But if you'll hop on my back, I'll be glad to give you a ride. I get *so* few visitors."

The tarantula seems friendly enough. But you're not sure you want to be alone with him in a long tunnel.

If you want to ride the tarantula through the tunnel, turn to page 62.

If you would rather climb to the top of the Tower of Spiders, excuse yourself politely and turn to page 88.

The smoke has almost cleared as you enter the cave. What you find inside looks something like the cottage that disappeared. There is a table with three place settings, and a steaming bowl at each place. But everything is three times larger than the cottage of the bears. And seated around the table are three dragons.

"My stew has no salt," complains Mama Dragon. She waddles to the hearth to fetch some.

"My stew is too cold," whines Baby Dragon. He puffs on his dish, and little flames erupt between his half-formed teeth.

"My stew has no *elf!*" roars Papa Dragon.

Three sets of beady eyes turn on you. Before you can disappear, you are enveloped in deadly dragon's breath.

THE END

58

The minute hand moves with clumsy jerks. Worried that you might fall, you choose the smooth-running hour hand, even though the ride to the window will take six hours.

You wait until 6:45, then leap from the rose trellis to grab hold of the gently gliding hand. It supports your weight well, and you are even able to doze.

Once an hour, you must flatten yourself against the clock face while the minute hand bounces by. But the ride goes smoothly.

Finally it is a few minutes before midnight—or noon, you cannot be sure. Sliding down the cast-iron arm of the hour hand, you are able to swing your legs through the oval window and rest on the rounded sill.

The window is the opening of a chute! At 12:00 you release your hold on the hour hand and slide down into darkness.

Turn to page 122.

60

from page 9

Determined to help your people, you decide to begin your quest in the Tower of Bones. On close examination, you see that the arch framing the doorway is made from the huge curved tusks of an ancient animal, while the door handle is probably the jawbone of some smaller beast, perhaps a boar.

Carefully avoiding the spiky teeth still lodged in the jawbone, you pull open the door and pass beneath the tusks.

You are faced with two sweeping staircases on each side of a spacious hall. Both staircases have banisters carved from some kind of enormous backbone.

Blocking the foot of the first staircase is a heap of discarded bones, the size of a haystack. You see that the pile is made of the fragile skeletons of hundreds of fish. At the foot of the second staircase is a similar pile, containing the bulky bones of doglike creatures—jackals or wolves.

If you want to climb the first staircase, turn to page 20.

If you want to climb the second staircase, turn to page 30.

You slide down the tunnel and land with a thud on a cold stone staircase. The manticore has vanished, and there are unbroken cobwebs everywhere. You must be in the Tower of Spiders.

Blazing torches flank an iron door on the staircase landing. And the stairs seem to continue up for several more flights.

If you want to search the room behind the iron door, turn to page 14.

If you prefer to climb to the top of the staircase, turn to page 88.

You decide that the tarantula has had plenty of opportunity to eat you if he'd wanted to, so you spring lightly onto his back.

"I hope this will lead to the magic herb," you say, holding your torch aloft to light the entrance to the tunnel. It is so narrow inside that the two of you just fit. As the bristly spider creeps along, you tell him the story of your quest.

"I am glad to help," says the sympathetic spider.

The tunnel continues for a long way, climbing neither up nor down. Gradually a light appears.

"We're almost to the end!" you say.

"But what is that?" asks the tarantula, as all at once the light is blocked out. He focuses his eight eyes on the exit. "It looks as though a giant's hand has covered the end of the tunnel."

The tarantula charges at the exit, sending your torch flying from your grip. As the fiery torch hurtles toward the exit, it lights the lines on the palm of a gigantic hand.

The burned hand pulls back, and the tarantula rushes through the uncovered exit, into the light of an oval room.

There is no giant—only a giant hand the size of the tarantula. It is lying palm up, and it seems to be recovering quickly from the slight burn.

"We must be in the Tower of Hands," you tell the tarantula. The enormous hand rolls over onto its fingers and begins to move like an angry spider.

"I can go no further, Lifin," says the tarantula. "There is a trap door in the floor. You must run for it. I can handle this hand."

The hand tightens into a fist and rushes at the tarantula as you leap to the ground. You pop through the trap door and pause to look back. The tarantula has his jaws fastened to one giant finger, and has flipped the hand over onto its knuckles. The hand struggles helplessly.

"Good luck!" calls the friendly spider.

Climbing down a rickety ladder, you arrive in a hand-shaped courtyard. You are faced with a single door.

Turn to page 40.

from page 119

You gather your remaining energy and close your eyes. Picturing the inside of a spiral seashell, you soon feel yourself spiraling away.

Weak and exhausted, lying flat on your stomach, you come to your senses. You are suspended on a sticky net, high above the stone floor of a musty tower room.

Suddenly the net begins to vibrate. Your limbs are stuck to the strands of the net, and it takes all of your strength just to lift your head. Then you are sorry you bothered.

An enormous hairy spider is picking its way through the net—its web! This is the last sight you see in the Tower of Spiders.

THE END

___

Even though the skull looks frightening, you decide to try your luck at the top.

Scrambling up a bony foot is like scaling a jagged cliff. An elven leap brings you safely to a kneecap, and from there you leap to the smooth white shelf of the hipbone.

You could spring to the rib cage, but you decide to climb an arm instead. Resting for a moment on the wide, flat collarbone, you venture a look at the skull that looms above you. The collarbone feels as strong and secure as the sunbaked clay of an elven path, but the enormous skull looks steep and perilous. Its jaws are closed. You will have to use the nostrils as handholds. And the faint light behind the empty eye sockets creates for the eyeless skull a gaze both remote and otherworldly.

Summoning thoughts of Elvir and your fading people, you leap once again. Gripping the nostril crevices, you vault inside the mysterious skull.

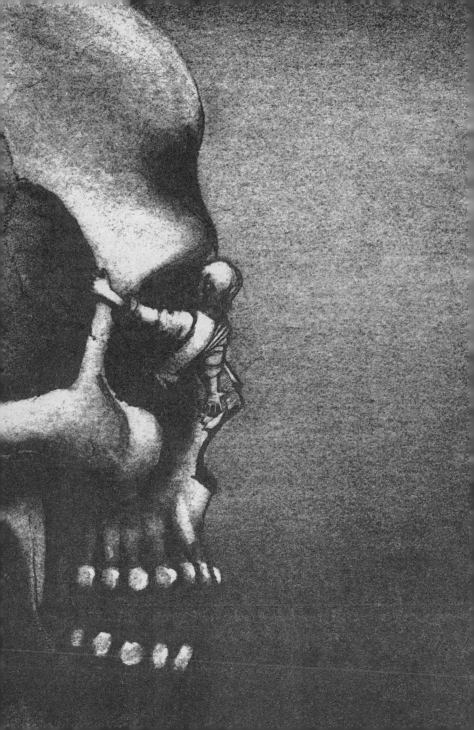

There is no floor! Flailing wildly, you grab for a piece of bone that hangs like a stalactite from the crest of the skull. A wishbone! And the ends of the wishbone are the sources of the glowing lights.

You have little time to wonder what a wishbone is doing inside a giant's skull, for you can feel the slender bone breaking under your weight.

Cccrraack! The wishbone snaps, and you slide along the back of the hollow skull. You grab for the spinal column, and tumble into a hole at its top. You are falling down a chute!

Turn to page 122.

68

Two pearls may be twice as useful as one, so you leave your newly won treasure on the ground and prepare to take another.

Dislodging the sturdy branch from the first oyster shell, you pull it quickly free as the huge oyster clamps shut. You drag the branch to a second shell, even larger than the first, and wedge it in.

This oyster holds a pearl with a pinkish cast, the color of first light. Nestled inside the giant shell, it looks as fragile as a soap bubble.

Swinging your legs over the side of the oyster shell, you slip and slide along its curved surface and try to grab the pink pearl. But as you try to stop yourself, the pearl shoots through your arms, uncovering a round opening in the floor of the shell. Into the hole you slide.

The flying pearl strikes the base of the branch and dislodges your wedge. The branch is falling, and the oyster shell is closing!

The slippery pearl skids back down the inside of the shell, knocking you farther into the opening in the floor, just as the oyster slams shut.

You are in a tunnel, sliding quickly away from the elf-eating oyster. You land in the darkness with a thump.

Turn to page 95.

from page 102

"Excuse me, Mr. Yeti," you say. "I can't stay and play today. But if you help me climb down into the hole, I will look for the ball you lost."

The yeti sniffles and nods gratefully.

The hole is at the center of the roof, where you had first seen the yeti kneeling like a furry white cone. The hole seems to lead to a chute of some kind, and you think you can see a colorful toy ball stuck in an elbow where the chute takes a turn. But the distance down to it is at least three times your height.

"Let me tie one of your hairs around my waist," you suggest. "Then you can lower me down."

The yeti dutifully yanks one of the long, coarse hairs that grow from his head down to his feet. It is as thick as yak rope, and you are sure it will hold.

"Lower me slowly, and don't let go," you instruct the yeti. Sliding into the chute, you soon reach the lost ball.

"Here it comes!" you call, tossing the ball up and out of the mouth of the chute.

The yeti squeals with delight and reaches to catch his treasured toy as you plummet down the chute, forgotten.

Turn to page 122.

70

from page 95

You choose the door with the still-smoldering skull, and enter a room as dimly lit as the hallway you just left.

The walls are hidden behind curtains strung with small bones and assorted teeth. And the floor is made from arm bones and leg bones laid in neat rows.

Suddenly the curtains begin to click and clatter, and a chilling breeze fills the room. A cold white mist rises between the cracks in the bony floor. It's a ghost. The ghost of a giant skull!

The phantom skull grins, then moves toward you, gnashing its teeth. You can feel its icy breath as its jaws open wide. It seems to want to add *your* bones to its horrible collection.

If you turn and run from the skull, turn to page 105.

If you try to stop it with an elven spark, turn to page 118.

from page 52

Up and down and up again, your elven instincts take over and you jump in time to the hypnotic rhythms of the dervish song. You join a line of jumping spiders and circle the room.

Faster you jump and your circle moves faster, until your head begins to spin. You feel as if you are floating, and you can no longer tell the difference between up and down.

You are in a trance. You can no longer remember what you came here for, or where you are. You have misplaced your name. You jump, and jump, and jump.

THE END

from page 48

You choose the path to the flower arbor. Not even in the Great Meadow have you seen such unusual blossoms or smelled such strange perfumes. And the colors!

This is like standing under a rainbow, you think, stepping into the arbor. As blooms burst open, colors explode like fireworks against a sky of green.

You breathe deeply, enjoying the heady scent that fills the arbor. Feeling a delightful dizziness, you watch with fascination as a long green tendril disengages itself from the arbor to twine gently about your arm. A crimson flower spreads its petals to unfurl a snakelike tongue that licks your cheek. How friendly they are, you think.

The tendril tightens! The heads of flowers reach hungrily for your ears and your legs! Elftraps!

You pinch your nose closed against their intoxicating aroma. If you act quickly, you might be able to break away and run for the lake. Or, you can try to stun the elf-eating flowers with your elven spark.

If you try the elven spark, turn to page 54.

If you run for the lake, turn to page 90.

74

from page 86

You realize that each time the pounding fists multiply, they also shrink. You decide to wait until many small fists cover the floor.

Soon the floor is crowded with an ocean of small hammering fists. The room resounds with their rumbling, like the clomping boots of a hundred marching goblins.

Skipping and jumping, you hop deftly from one rising fist to the next, like a frog on a rippling bed of lily pads. In no time, you zigzag to the mouth of the tunnel and step through the arched entrance.

Taking a few steps into the tunnel, you are quickly engulfed in shadows. You wonder what an Automaton Tunnel is as you feel your way along the thick stone walls.

Gradually you notice a whirring sound, and a curved wall ahead of you is struck by a circular beam of light. The whirring sound grows louder and the light beam grows stronger. Could a train be approaching? You see no tracks.

Flattening yourself against the cool stone wall, you wait. The beam of light splashes around the corner, momentarily blinding you.

Then you see that it *is* a headlight. But it is mounted on the knuckles of a huge mechanical hand! Its robot arm twists through the tunnel like a long steel accordion, and its fingers open and close with a series of metallic clicks.

The strange machine hesitates, then turns toward you. You back away a step, and the automatic arm moves forward.

You turn to run, but the automaton plucks you off your feet with its thumb and forefinger. It whisks you backward through the tunnel at a frightening clip.

Suddenly the tunnel branches, and the robot arm whirs to a stop at the crossing. A rattling sound comes from the other branch, and you see in the headlight of the automaton a skeletal arm reaching to meet you!

The two hands trade their cargo—one Lifin, helpless elf—and the giant bony hand deposits you at the end of the tunnel, facing a bone-handled door. The hand nudges you toward the door, then withdraws into the darkness of the tunnel. Suddenly, the bony handle turns and the door opens onto a dark hallway. You must have been passed through to the Tower of Bones!

Turn to page 95.

76

Swinging the leg bone with all of your might, you crash it down onto the head of the attacking skeleton.

The bone splinters on the jackal's thick skull, then crumbles to a fine white dust.

The stunned jackal bellows, and staggers toward the staircase. He seems resolved to guard the stairs, and is quickly recovering from the blow you have given him.

If you hurry to the first stairway in the Tower of Bones, turn to page 20.

If you think you had better disappear, turn to page 44.

from page 28

The widow's magical webbing has wrapped you in a cocoon of threads like an elven mummy. Struggling has only made the trap grow tighter, so you hold perfectly still, your arms at your sides.

"Oh, my," says the spider. "It's been such a long time since I've had a tasty young elf!" She resumes her song and begins an eight-legged waltz around the room.

Now is your chance! You are able to wiggle your fingers freely, so you test the spark. Gathering your four fingertips together to form a single surface, you brush them lightly with your thumb. An elven spark crackles from your fingertips and singes a layer of the fine, silken threads. It works!

"What was that?" sniffs the widow, creeping toward you. A slight burning smell hovers about the melted strands of the web. But you have a distraction planned.

Pretending to struggle, you fall onto your back and roll toward the door, careful to avoid any thrashing motion that may tighten the web.

"*Hee, hee*, you won't get far," the widow cackles. "My web will hug you closer the harder you fight."

You have reached the door. Instantly you send a shower of sparks from each hand. The silken webbing sizzles, and you leap free! The widow is quick, but you dash out of the room, slamming the door on your poisonous captor.

Turn to page 52.

78

from page 104/from page 110

You decide to climb to the snowy mountain peak. Wind whistles in your sensitive ears, and you shiver with the sudden cold.

But as you reach the mountaintop, you understand where you must be in this Tower of Tricks. Ahead of you is an enormous cone, covered in white fur—the spire at the top of the Tower of Beasts. And as soon as you have seen through the illusion, the mountain landscape disappears.

You are next to a low wall at the top of the Tower of Beasts. But the furry cone is moving! It doubles in height and lets out a wail. It's a yeti—an abominable snowman! And he is wailing at *you!*

You are close enough to the edge to leap safely across to the next tower. You can see from the teeth around its edge that it must be the Tower of Eaters. Or you can try to outrun the lumbering yeti.

If you leap to the Tower of Eaters, turn to page 25.

If you decide to outrun the yeti, turn to page 102.

80

You decide to scale the garden wall next to the trellis of grabber roses.

Leaping over the snapping flower beds, you narrowly miss being grabbed by the huge, mittlike hands of a nearby tulip tree. Geranium hands punch at you like red fists, while the skinny fingers of what once were spider mums snatch at your ankles like angry dogs.

A final leap brings you safely to the garden wall, and you clamber up the rough-hewn stone, beyond the reach of the garden grabbers.

At first you climb easily, until you are high above the garden, halfway to the clock. But soon it becomes no easy task to find handholds and footholds, for the stone blocks have been polished as smooth as glass. You are forced to edge closer and closer to the trellis of roses that leads to the clock.

The thorns on the rose stems are your least worry. Each fragrant bloom has turned into a perfumed hand, of palest yellow, ruby red, or creamy white. They reach for you, and you pull away, searching for a place to wedge your foot. Your foot slips! You scramble desperately for a handhold on the face of the slippery wall.

Suddenly something breaks your fall! A rose-pink hand has caught your own outstretched hand, and is hauling you to safety on the trellis. A yellow hand takes your elbow and pulls you higher. These grabbers seem to be helping hands!

You climb hand over hand to the bottom of the enormous clock. Half moon and half sun, the clock face smiles blankly. The hands point to 6:30, but you can't tell if it is day or night. The little oval window, wide open but dark, lies beneath the 12.

How can you reach the window? The roses trail off, and the wall around you is as smooth as ice.

Straining, you can just reach the hands of the clock. Their long cast-iron arms point accusingly at the symbols of time.

The longer hand jumps. It is the minute hand, on its thirty-stop route to the 12. In another five minutes it will be out of your reach!

If you decide to ride the minute hand, turn to page 115.

If you would rather take the hour hand, turn to page 58.

82

Jumping to your feet, you begin to dance. You are not sure you are doing the tarantella, but you hope that any lively dance will overcome the tarantula's poison.

You leap and twirl, avoiding the hairy spider, who is gazing at you from the corner near the tunnel. Faster and faster you spin, springing on your hands like an acrobat.

Finally, exhausted, you pause to rest.

"Bravo! Bravo!" cries the tarantula, clicking his claws. "A masterful performance!"

You eye the spider suspiciously. "Is it time for your lunch?" you demand. "Am I poisoned enough?"

"Don't be silly," replies the spider. "Tarantulas don't eat elves. And we're rarely poisonous. I just gave you a harmless little nip so you'd stop throwing that torch around. You were making me nervous."

"I'm sorry if the fire frightened you," you say.

"Well, if you keep the torch away from me, I'll give you a ride through the tunnel," says the spider, "in return for your entertaining dancing."

The tarantula's offer seems friendly enough. But you're not sure you want to be alone with him in a long tunnel. What if he decides to eat you after all?

If you decide to ride the tarantula through the tunnel, turn to page 62.

If you would rather climb to the top of the Tower of Spiders, turn to page 88.

from page 108

You dive into the huge magic lamp, fighting off the demon elf-eaters with slaps and sparks. Wounded and exhausted, you manage to close the lid. You are too weak to disappear.

Outside, in the windowless and doorless room, the gleeful demons wait for you. Inside the lamp, you are awkwardly curled into an elf-ball.

You feel some kind of friction in your body. The elf-eaters are rubbing the lamp! You find you are growing more comfortable. You are shrinking! Spiky teeth spring from your gums, and your elven fingers sprout claws.

Flying from the lamp, you rejoice in your freedom as the thirteenth demon.

THE END

84

from page 41

Lunging quickly, you wrestle the long sewing needle from the spider's grasp and spin away before she can grab you.

The angry widow whirls the cloak about her head and casts it like a fisherman's net. Through the air it sails, flapping hungrily toward you like a great green bat.

Springing out of the way, you catch the cloak on the tip of the needle and fling it back at the spider.

The widow shrieks in fury and sidesteps to avoid the flying cloak. You hold the needle before you like a sword, ready to do battle.

The spider moves closer, watching you with steely eyes. You back away, fending her off with your makeshift sword, until you bump into a wall. To your left is a bubbling vat of dye, and to your right a spinning wheel.

The widow attacks! Using all of your strength, you overturn the vat of hot dye, staining the floor a vivid purple. The widow reaches for your head, her fangs dripping poison. But her eight legs slip and slide in the oily dye. She crashes against you, pinning your arm to the wall. With a freezing wail of pain, she vanishes into thin air, your sewing needle piercing her heart.

Shaken, you retreat down the passage the way you came. Looking back, you see that the hallway is crawling with tiny spiders. Ahead of you is the stone staircase.

Turn to page 106.

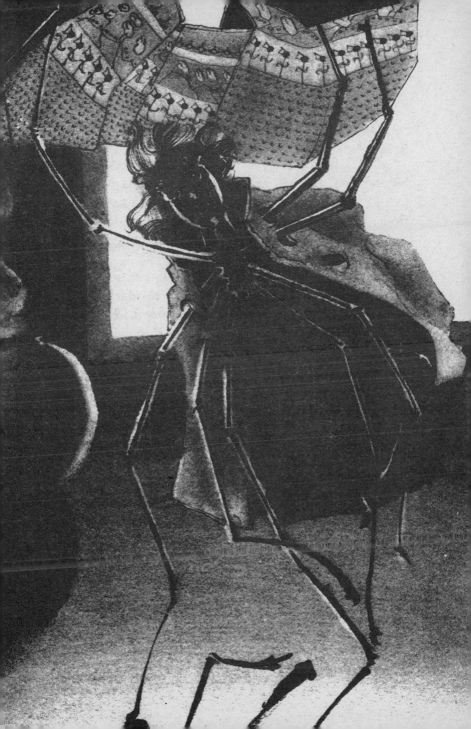

86

from page 12

You race through the door at the end of the aisle, heedless of the pounding noise.

You stop, however, as soon as the door clicks behind you, for before you is an enormous pounding fist. It fills the otherwise empty room and pounds the floor. Ka-*boom!* Ka-*boom!* With each relentless blow, the floor shakes and your teeth rattle. If you get caught under it, you will surely be crushed.

As the fist raises and lowers, you can see that it blocks an open archway, leading to darkness. It reminds you of a railroad tunnel. Ka-*boom!* Ka-*boom!* As the fist goes up, you can see a sign next to the archway: CAUTION: AUTOMATON TUNNEL.

Planning to dash to the tunnel the moment the great fist begins to rise, you take a careful step into the room. But as the huge hand pounds the floor, it suddenly splits into two smaller fists. Ka-*boom*-ka, ka-*boom*-ka! Then four. Ka-*boom*-boom, ka-*boom*-boom-*boom!* Eight. Sixteen fists!

You cover your ears against the thunderous clamor of thirty-two, then sixty-four hammering fists.

If you want to try to get to the tunnel, turn to page 74.

If you'd rather disappear, turn to page 44.

from page 100

Wondering if the rare plant you seek could be in the pirate's treasure chest, you accept his offer to peek.

"Come here then, matey," says the buccaneer with a proud grin. "I'll show ye something the like of which ye'll never again see."

You stand in front of the chest, which reaches higher than your waist, and hold your breath as the pirate throws back the heavy lid. But you see only darkness—the chest is empty.

"Look closely, matey," says the pirate. Leaning over the edge of the chest for a better look, you suddenly feel a shove. You tumble headlong into the bottomless treasure chest. You are falling!

The pirate's booming laughter follows you down the dark, eerie tunnel. Far above you, the lid to the treasure chest slams, and you continue to fall in silence.

Turn to page 11.

from pages 56/61/82/106

Up you climb until you come to a door. You open the door and smell fresh air. Delighted, you walk out onto a vast open turret.

You are on a wide, round roof, the size of an archery field. The turret is ringed by a wall. From where you stand, in the center of the roof, you can see the Tower of Beasts to one side, and the Tower of Hands to the other. But your attention is drawn to a different view.

You cross the turret to the far side, away from the other towers. It is late afternoon, and the Great Meadow is a lazy green quilt, patterned with flowers. In the distance you can just see the delicate dwellings of your elven village.

Exploring the turret, you see that the edge of each tower touches the next. You could easily leap to a neighboring turret. And while there seems to be a flagstone courtyard far below, between the five towers, you can see no magic plants there. You also find an opening in the roof, a chute, but you can't tell where it leads.

Suddenly you notice a huge green spider on your turret next to the Tower of Hands. He is spinning a thread of silk—a silken lasso!

You had better get away fast. You can jump down the chute, and hope that it doesn't end in this spider's nest. Or you can try to leap across to the Tower of Beasts.

If you want to slide down the chute, turn to page 122.

If you want to leap to the Tower of Beasts, turn to page 94.

90

You head for the lake, hoping to find an easy route to the earth mound. But the path ends abruptly at a narrow strip of sand, and the lake is surrounded by boulders.

Sunlight sparkles on the gently rippling surface of the little lake. But you are dismayed, for most elves are poor swimmers, and you are no exception.

Noticing a flat gray object wedged next to a rock, you walk to the end of the beach to investigate. A raft!

The logs of the raft are weathered and coated with lichen, but the thongs that bind them together seem secure. And tied to one edge is a long sapling that should serve as a pole if the lake is not too deep.

It would certainly be quicker to pole the raft to the far side of the lake than it would be to climb across the jagged boulders. But you do hate the water. What if the raft leaks?

If you decide to take the raft, turn to page 50.

If you would rather climb across the rocks, turn to page 13.

from page 103

The ribs are easier to reach than the grimacing skull, and somehow less scary.

An elven leap brings you to a bony kneecap. From there you shimmy easily to the broad hipbone, as wide and as smooth as an alabaster ship.

Trying not to think about where you are, you catch your breath and prepare to leap again. A final effort, and your fingers curl about the lowermost rib, as thick as a birch sapling.

Swinging yourself up, you are able to vault into the cavity of the great breastbone. You are surprised to find a wooden platform suspended at the center of the ribs.

Why is this platform here? you wonder. The floor of the hall looks miles away. Still far above you is the floating roof of a pearly jawbone.

Suddenly you understand the reason for the little platform. With a heaving creak, the heavy ribs crash together around you, encircling you with bony bars.

You are trapped in a rib cage. And there is no escape.

THE END

from page 40

You choose the room with the whistling sounds. To enter, you must turn the finger that is poked through the keyhole. It feels dry and cold.

You enter an elegant room, filled with delicate furniture and art objects. The room appears to be unoccupied.

Picking up a crystal statuette of a tree fairy, you delight in the rainbows it throws on the marble floor. Suddenly a whistling noise shoots past your ear, and a breeze ruffles your hair. You look up to see a white glove hovering above your head. It shakes a finger at you, then snatches the statuette and smashes it at your feet!

Another whistle, and something pinches you from behind. *Whizz!* A glove tweaks your ear and sails over your head. *Crash!* Several more empty gloves push an ornate urn from its place on the mantelpiece. *Zoom!* An ivory milkmaid barely misses your cheek!

You are being taunted by an army of poltergeist evening gloves!

If you try to fend them off with the elven spark, turn to page 16.

If you want to try to catch a pair and put them on, turn to page 107.

94

from page 89

You leap to the turret of the Tower of Beasts, rolling onto the rooftop just in time to avoid the green spider's spinning lasso.

You have landed on a circular parapet. At the center of the rooftop is a cone-shaped spire, covered in brilliant white fur. You walk around it, looking for a door.

But the furry cone shudders, and doubles in height! It is moving! It is a *yeti*—an "abominable snowman"—and he is wailing at the sight of you!

You are close enough to leap to the next tower. You can tell from the teeth around its edge that it must be the Tower of Eaters. Or you can try to outrun the lumbering yeti and search for a door.

If you leap to the Tower of Eaters, turn to page 25.

If you decide to outrun the yeti, turn to page 102.

from pages 33/49/68/75/121

At the end of a spooky hallway stands a pair of identical doors. They are wooden and plain, except for one unusual feature. In front of each door hovers a ghostly ball of pale yellow light.

As you move closer, the balls of light begin to pulse and change shape. You can feel their warmth. One globe takes the shape of a grinning skull. The other becomes a crossbones—both traditional danger warnings.

Now the deathly images press against the doors, burning like hot irons into the ancient wood. After a moment they vanish, leaving two charred brands.

You look from the door with the skull brand to the door with the crossbones. How far away the Great Meadow seems from this dismal hallway in the Tower of Bones!

If you open the skull door, turn to page 70.

If you choose the door with the crossbones, turn to page 100.

96

from page 102

You decide that the yeti is lonely and just wants a friend to play with.

"Yeti!" you call from a safe distance away. "Do you want to play hide-and-seek with me?"

"Oh, yes, Elf!" The yeti stops crying at once. "I am too big to hide, though. So you will have to hide, and then I will seek you, and then I can eat you, yes?"

Hmm. You've never heard of a rule like that before. But you have a plan.

"All right," you say. "You must close your eyes and count to one hundred and one."

"One....two....three...." the yeti counts. You search the roof for an exit. "Forty-five, forty-six...." Nothing! Your plan is not working!

You circle the rooftop once more, and finally peer into the hole at the center. It appears to be a tunnel of some kind, but your view is blocked by the yeti's toy ball.

"No peeking!" you tell the monster, as you lower yourself into the tunnel.

"One hundred and one! Here I come!" hollers the yeti, as you kick the ball loose. You plummet into a pit filled with yeti food, and long yeti fingers are reaching for you already.

It looks like you had better disappear after all. And fast!

Turn to page 18.

You decide that you have been lucky so far. One pearl is enough. You like to have at least one hand free in case of emergencies.

With your trusty pearl tucked snugly under your arm, you enter the earth mound in the Tower of Eaters.

You are in a storeroom. Against one wall is an empty suit of armor, just your size. A great deal of noise is coming from beyond a door in the opposite wall. It sounds like the clatter of a gnome's armory, metal striking metal in regular beats.

If you follow the noise, turn to page 112.

If you want to dress in the armor first, turn to page 38.

from page 35

Leaping over the cluster of snapping hands, you run for the garden door. Hands grab at you from every direction. Some have fernlike claws and mossy fur. Others are gnarled like tree roots.

Leaping over a hand-waving hedge, you swerve to avoid a grasping azalea, then leap over a bed of marigolds and clinging violets. Your last leap has taken you under the limbs of a sassafras tree. Suddenly two powerful grabbers lift you into the air. One hand grips your left shoulder and another your right ankle.

You dangle in their hold, frustratingly close to the garden door.

If you try to use the elven spark to shock the grabbers into dropping you, turn to page 29.

If you want to disappear, turn to page 119.

from page 37

You don't want to dance near a hungry spider, so you decide to disappear. You can dance the tarantella wherever you land next.

Gathering all of your energy, you close your eyes and imagine the inside of a spiral seashell. Soon you feel your slight elven body spiraling away.

You open your eyes in a dim room, no bigger than a large closet. The tarantula is nowhere in sight. Overcome with weakness, as Elvir had warned, you collapse to the floor. I must *dance*, you tell yourself, I *must*.

The hall is so narrow that you can rest your back against one wall and reach forward to touch the other. Using the walls for leverage, you manage to pull yourself to your feet.

I *must* dance, you think, jumping feebly into the air. But your collar catches on a hook in the wall, and you hang in midair, weak and helpless.

Your limbs slowly grow numb as the tarantula's poison does its work. You try to tear your collar from the hook, but your arms feel just too heavy.

As your eyes adjust to the darkness, you can see that you are indeed in a long closet. You must be in the Tower of Bones. For there are several other hooks along the wall—and a skeleton is hanging from each one.

THE END

100

The burned-in crossbones are still smoking slightly as you push open the wooden door. You enter a damp cavern that smells of the sea. Sand crunches beneath your soft boots, and bleached white seashells litter the floor, the cast-off skeletons of small marine creatures.

At the center of the cave is a massive wooden sea chest.

"Yo ho, matey!" thunders a voice from a shadowed corner. You look up with a start.

A bearded pirate steps out of the darkness and winks at you with his visible eye. The other eye is covered with a plain black patch, and he wears a tattered vest over knee-length breeches. A golden earring gleams in his ear. On his hat are emblazoned two crossed bones.

"I suppose ye'll be after me treasure," says the pirate, indicating the chest. "Well, I'll be tarred and feathered before I'll let anybody take it from *me!* But I'll let ye have a look if ye like!"

If you peek into the treasure chest, turn to page 87.

If you refuse the pirate's offer, turn to page 111.

102

You run from the yeti at elven speed. He is so big and clumsy compared to a fleet-footed elf that you are able to lead him on a merry chase around the tower. But you can find no sign of an exit on this rooftop.

The yeti lumbers after you, around and around. So nimbly do you leap back and forth that the slow-moving yeti gets confused. He finally sits down with a thump at the center of the roof. Tears of frustration fill his eyes, and soon he is weeping, soaking his fur. He chokes out words in his gruff voice.

"It isn't fair, it just isn't *fair*," he sobs. "First I drop my favorite ball down this stupid hole. And then a visitor who comes to play runs away from me. Wooooh, booo hoooo, what a *beastly* day!"

If you decide to play with the yeti while you look for an escape route, turn to page 96.

If you offer to retrieve his ball, turn to page 69.

Or you can disappear. Turn to page 18.

You dash out the door and run down several hallways. When you reach a room with a high ceiling, you pause breathlessly. Luckily you are no longer being followed. But you are lost somewhere within the Tower of Bones.

Then you notice him. Rising before you, its eerie head reaching to the rafters, is the motionless skeleton of a giant man.

You are attracted to a glow between its ribs, and to a faint light behind its hollow eye sockets.

The bones look easy to climb, and you have nowhere else to go.

If you climb to the space between the skeleton's ribs, turn to page 91.

If you head for the light behind its eyes, turn to page 65.

104

from page 47

You have to think quickly. Almost everyone has two eyes—that's no help. Pointed ears? Foxes have pointed ears, it's true, but so do many beasts. And goblins. Even elves! Elves don't have a long tail, though. But my *tale* of adventure is certainly long enough. And there are two "I's" in my name! L*i*f*i*n! If I guess "myself," I *will* be the cleverest of beasts!

"The answer to your riddle, great Sphinx," you reply, "is LIFIN."

"And so it is, young elf." The sphinx opens her wings to unveil a looking-glass. You are delighted to see that you are your elven self once again.

The desert fades, and the sphinx with it. Suddenly you are standing on the side of a mountain, an hour's climb from the snow-capped peak.

Turn to page 78.

You try to run, but the bones in the floor roll under your feet like logs or barrels. The ghost skull laughs wickedly. You run and run, but you are getting nowhere. It is all you can do just to keep your balance.

The skull swoops down at you, its teeth chattering with the sound of breaking ice.

Veering to one side, you duck out of its way, but your boot catches on one of the rolling bones, and you fall!

The swooping ghost passes through the treacherous floor behind you as you struggle to sit up. Feeling a frigid wind surround you, you jump to your feet. The skull is rising from the floor beneath you!

You try to leap away, but you are too late. You are trapped in the freezing teeth of the phantom skull.

With the braying noise of a winter wind, you are sucked into its ghostly mouth and swallowed. Down you slide into a dark tunnel that must once have been the throat of the phantom skull.

Turn to page 119.

106

You head for the staircase leading up through the tower, and reach the first step safely, trailing cobwebs from your shoulders and elbows.

A glance behind you renews your fears, however. The hundreds of "harmless little spiders" have gathered into a million-legged mass and are moving toward you. You are hopelessly outnumbered!

What elven ability will help me now? you wonder, as you flee in leaps and bounds up the stone staircase.

Pausing at a landing to look back, you realize with relief that your natural elven talent for leaping has brought you well out of range of the sea of spiders, who are struggling to scale the second stair.

The staircase seems to continue for several more stories. On the next landing, however, is an iron door flanked by blazing torches.

If you want to open the iron door, turn to page 14.

If you decide to climb to the top of the tower, turn to page 88.

from page 92

The gloves whisk madly through the air, smashing statues and overturning fragile tables, pulling your hair and tugging your clothes.

You miss grabbing one glove as it flies by, but you are able to catch the jeweled butterfly it drops.

Suddenly two gloves clap themselves over your eyes. This may be your chance.

In an instant you thrust your hands into the pair of gloves and pull them from your eyes. The other flying gloves applaud, and flit around the room like leaves in a whirlwind.

But what is this urge you have to smash things? Like this tea set? *Crash!* This ugly vase—you hurl it against the wall. This mirror—*shatter!* Let's tear the tapestries! *Yes!* Break the chairs! *Yes!* Topple the china cabinet! *Yes! Yes!*

"I won't stop until the Towers are piles of dust!" you cry, and set to your new task.

THE END

108

Down you tumble, landing with a thud on a pile of thick rugs.

You are in a room with no windows or doors. The rugs on the floor are patterned with fruits and other kinds of food. And the walls are painted with scenes of feasting, suitable for the Tower of Eaters.

There is no furniture at all, except for a huge, battered brass lamp, of the shape you have read about in elven tales. A genie's lamp!

You have nowhere to go, so you rub the lamp.

But it is not a genie who streams from the lamp. Instead, twelve demons, each the size of your arm, spring forth one by one, smacking their lips and sneering. They snap at you with their sharp teeth.

You recognize these creatures from the lore of the elves—but you always thought they were just myths. They are elf-eaters, and they are *deadly*.

If you try to protect yourself by climbing inside the big lamp, turn to page 83.

If you disappear, turn to page 17.

110

You are as hungry as a bear, so you sit down to eat your porridge, hoping you can finish your meal before Mama Bear and Papa Bear show up.

Your porridge is still steaming hot, so you blow into your dish to cool it. The steam swirls all around you, making clouds so thick that you can no longer see Goldilocks or the cottage.

You begin to cough. These clouds are not steam, they are smoke! And they stink of dragon's breath!

Coughing and choking, you back away from the billowing smoke, feeling for the cottage door. But the cottage has vanished. As the smoke clears, you see that you are standing in the mouth of a cave. A rough dirt path leads far above you to a snowy mountain peak.

You realize with relief that your bear's head is gone, and that your hands are once again your own.

If you want to explore the cave, turn to page 57.

If you want to climb to the mountain peak, turn to page 78.

The winking pirate seems nice enough, but you do not quite trust him.

"No thank you, sir," you say politely. "I have no wish to see any treasure save the one I seek."

"And what may that be?" the pirate asks. "Jewels? A kingdom? A partner in marriage, perhaps?"

"I seek an herb, a simple plant," you reply cautiously.

"Ahhhh, a *plant!*" says the pirate. "Why, just such a plant grows at the bottom of my chest. Jump in and take a look for yourself. You're welcome to it!"

The pirate throws open the heavy lid of the chest, and you see that it is filled with bones. You suspect a trick. He must want to shut you inside the chest.

"I could not bear to disturb your beautiful bones," you tell the pirate, walking toward the door.

"*Aaarrggh,*" growls the fierce buccaneer. "Then I'll disturb them for you!" And with that he grabs a heavy bone from the chest. Wielding it like a cudgel, he chases you to the door. You run as fast as you can.

Turn to page 103.

112

You step onto a catwalk in a cavernous room and cover your ears against the banging and pounding.

But what is this? You are moving. You are standing on a rotating belt, and it is bearing you toward a gigantic machine, high above the floor of the room.

Looking down, you understand. You must have entered some kind of cannery in the Tower of Eaters. Mechanical arms are working, assembly-line fashion, to fill the cans on a moving belt below you.

One after another, the arms grab objects from the belt you stand on and cram them into waiting cans below. They pack apples and tomatoes, beetles and shrubs. Each can is neatly labeled. You gulp as you catch sight of the large can riding along below *you:* CANNED ELF—*16 lbs.*

As you approach the mechanical arms, you see one of them reject a rotten grapefruit and toss it into a hole in the floor. An alarm sounds above the din of the machinery, and attendants swarm into the cannery. Ogres!

It is your turn to be canned! But as the mechanical arm reaches for you, you leap for the hole in the floor, leaving your treasured pearl in your place on the assembly line. The pearl is canned, no alarm sounds, and you fall into an evil-smelling tunnel.

Turn to page 119.

You are curious, but you decide to do as Goldilocks said.

"I must deliver this basket to Grandmother's house," you tell the manticore.

"Well, if you won't open it, *I will*," the manticore declares, snatching the basket from your clumsy paws.

"Hey, wait!" you say. But it is too late. The manticore places the basket on the ground and whips the blue-and-white cloth away. He gasps!

Then, in the blink of an eye, the beast dives head-first into the basket and disappears!

Hurrying to the basket, you too look inside. The basket has no bottom, and leads to a tunnel in the forest floor. There is no sign of the manticore.

If you follow the manticore into the tunnel, turn to page 61.

If you want to look for Grandmother's house empty-handed, turn to page 42.

114

from page 41

The widow's fangs glint with droplets of poison as she reaches for you.

In a flash you yank the cloak from the spider's grasp and hurl it over her head.

The cloak becomes a sticky web, as strong as steel wire. The widow thrashes and struggles, but the web only grows tighter. She is caught in her own trap!

You hate to hear a spider shriek, and she may have other magic spells, so you return to the passageway to continue your quest elsewhere.

Turn to page 52.

The minute hand jumps again. At precisely 6:33 you leap from the rose trellis and grab hold of the cast-iron finger. It is more delicate than you expected, and you are hanging many stories above the garden of grabbers.

You try to shimmy up the slender arm toward the center of the clock, but the angle is too steep and the arm is too flimsy, so you decide to stay where you are.

The arm lurches upward to 6:34. The jagged motion sends a tremor through the minute hand, and it vibrates in your grip. You lose your grip and fall!

Below you is a grasping bed of wild tiger lilies, testing their claws. You wish you had chosen the slow but steady hour hand.

THE END

116

The manticore is an annoying fellow, but he somehow doesn't seem dangerous. And you *are* curious. You decide to open the basket.

Awkwardly lifting the corner of the blue-and-white cloth with your furry paw, you are ready to peek inside when something springs from the basket with a *whoosh!* You are knocked off your feet, and the basket goes flying.

Momentarily stunned, you watch the former occupant of your picnic basket fluff her fur and ruffle her wings. She is a griffin, with the wings, claws, and beak of an eagle, and the body of a lioness.

The griffin angrily faces the manticore.

"How dare you interrupt my journey, Manticore?" she demands.

"Do you dare to challenge me yet again, Griffin?" the manticore growls.

The two beasts circle one another, ready to do battle. The griffin kicks the empty basket into a clump of bushes.

If you try to settle their dispute, turn to page 120.

If you want to look for Grandmother's house, empty-handed, turn to page 42.

118

The ghostly death's-head descends, shrieking wildly and breathing a frozen mist.

Gathering your fingertips together to make a single surface, you run your thumb lightly across them with a flick of your wrist. A fiery spark escapes from the end of your hand and flies into the face of the phantom skull!

Zzzzzt! The spark hits the ghost's front tooth with a sizzle. To your delight, the tooth quickly melts like a shard of ice in a fire.

Zzzzzt! Zzzzzt! In rapid succession, you aim your sparks at the ghost's gaping mouth. One after another, you strike its teeth. Soon the ghost is as toothless as a chicken.

"Greeeeee!" it shrieks in alarm. The tooth-and-bone curtains clatter and separate. Suddenly the room is filled with a hoard of angry, rattling skeletons.

This time you *run!*

Turn to page 103.

You plummet through a slimy hole, falling helplessly. Tumbling with you are various insects and strange-looking vegetables. Below you, steam rises from a dimly lit space.

Plop! You land with a splash in a bubbling cauldron. It is a stew pot! Just before you lose consciousness, you see a group of big, hungry ogres sharpening their knives and forks.

Several minutes later, you awaken, feeling sunburned, in the middle of a silver platter, surrounded by potatoes. A noisy feast is in progress.

You are the main course at an ogre's banquet in the Tower of Eaters!

But you are not cooked yet.

"Wait!" you cry. "I'm still raw!"

The ogres fall silent. Then they begin to laugh at the sight of a half-cooked elf.

If you think you can distract them with elven stories, turn to page 21.

If you would rather chance a disappearance, turn to page 64.

Perhaps you can stop this fight before it begins. You decide to take advantage of your new bear's head and let out a fierce growl.

"*Grrrrr!* Stop it, you two!" you command.

"Keep out of this, Bear-head," says the manticore.

"Who does he think he is, interrupting our weekly match?" asks the griffin.

Snarling and hissing, their teeth and claws bared and their eyes narrowed in fury, both beasts turn to attack *you!*

You are no match for a griffin and a manticore. You had better disappear right away.

Turn to page 11.

from page 30

Bracing yourself to bear the weight of the attacking jackal, you take careful aim, holding the leg bone upright. If you miss, you could lose an arm, for the skeleton jackal still has all of his teeth!

The bony beast leaps at your throat, and you jam the leg bone between his powerful jaws. It holds! With the bone lodged in his mouth, he is unable to bite.

The jackal howls and stumbles away, one leg incomplete.

You hurry up the staircase, eager to continue your quest.

Turn to page 95.

122

from pages 21/58/67/69/89

You slide down the dank, slippery chute. But you do not pick up too much speed, for the chute zigzags back and forth, breaking your fall into a series of gentle twists and turns. I must be falling the entire length of the tower, you think.

Finally you slide out of the chute and land with a thump on a soft bed of moss.

You are in a rocky cavern at the edge of a small lagoon. In the middle of the lagoon is a tiny island, on which grows a single leafy plant. And the plant emits a greenish light.

It can be only one thing—the magic herb! You must have found the secret route to the center of the Forbidden Towers!

There is no walkway to the little island, and the water looks murky and dangerous. You may be able to leap across the water if you take a running start. The larger problem is: how will you ever get back to your village with the plant?

You have only seconds to think, however, before a legion of spiders suddenly drop from their webs in the cavernous heights. And skeleton soldiers advance from the inky depths of the lagoon! Taloned hands reach forth from the cavern walls, and flying beasts hover above you. Elf-eaters drop from the chute, their mouths watering. One lands on your head!

Shutting your eyes against these horrors, you run, and you *spring*.

"Spiders, Hands, Bones, Eaters, Beasts, *begone!*" you scream as you leap through the air to the little island.

The noise is awful—shrieks and hollers, yells and shouts, crumbling and crashing—the likes of which you have never heard. Keeping your eyes squeezed tightly shut, you embrace something soothing and cool—the magic plant.

Finally, as the last faint wail dies away, you open your eyes. You are crouched at the center of the Great Meadow, your face buried in the broad leaves of the sweet-smelling herb. The sun is shining, and there is no trace of the monsters or the Forbidden Towers. They have all vanished.

Hundreds of elves are gathered at the edge of your village. But they are so pale and weak that you cry out in alarm. Are you too late? Are they ghosts? One by one they draw closer. Their color returns as they walk, then run to your side.

The elf-folk form a circle around you, breathing deeply of the healing plant's scent.

Elvir watches the celebration from one side of the circle. As his eyes meet yours, he beams even more as the elves of your village cluster around, lifting you to their shoulders.

"Hooray for Lifin!" they cry. "Finest of elves!"

THE END